the B

G

in

THE BIG
BAD WOLF

TEXT AND ILLUSTRATIONS COPYRIGHT © 2019 BY AARON BLABEY

ALL RIGHTS RESERVED. PUBLISHED BY SCHOLASTIC INC., *PUBLISHERS SINCE 1920,*
557 BROADWAY, NEW YORK, NY 10012. scholastic AND ASSOCIATED LOGOS ARE TRADEMARKS
AND/OR REGISTERED TRADEMARKS OF SCHOLASTIC INC. THIS EDITION PUBLISHED
UNDER LICENSE FROM SCHOLASTIC AUSTRALIA PTY LIMITED.
FIRST PUBLISHED BY SCHOLASTIC AUSTRALIA PTY LIMITED IN 2019.

THE PUBLISHER DOES NOT HAVE ANY CONTROL OVER AND DOES NOT ASSUME ANY
RESPONSIBILITY FOR AUTHOR OR THIRD-PARTY WEBSITES OR THEIR CONTENT.

NO PART OF THIS PUBLICATION MAY BE REPRODUCED, STORED IN A RETRIEVAL SYSTEM,
OR TRANSMITTED IN ANY FORM OR BY ANY MEANS, ELECTRONIC, MECHANICAL,
PHOTOCOPYING, RECORDING, OR OTHERWISE, WITHOUT WRITTEN PERMISSION OF THE PUBLISHER.
FOR INFORMATION REGARDING PERMISSION, WRITE TO SCHOLASTIC AUSTRALIA,
AN IMPRINT OF SCHOLASTIC AUSTRALIA PTY LIMITED, 345 PACIFIC HIGHWAY,
LINDFIELD NSW 2070 AUSTRALIA.

THIS BOOK IS A WORK OF FICTION. NAMES, CHARACTERS, PLACES, AND INCIDENTS ARE
EITHER THE PRODUCT OF THE AUTHOR'S IMAGINATION OR ARE USED FICTITIOUSLY, AND ANY
RESEMBLANCE TO ACTUAL PERSONS, LIVING OR DEAD, BUSINESS ESTABLISHMENTS,
EVENTS, OR LOCALES IS ENTIRELY COINCIDENTAL.

ISBN 978-1-338-30581-4

10 9 8 7 6 5 4 3 2 1   19 20 21 22 23

PRINTED IN THE U.S.A.   23
FIRST U.S. PRINTING 2019

· AARON BLABEY ·

the BAD GUYS

in

THE BIG
BAD WOLF

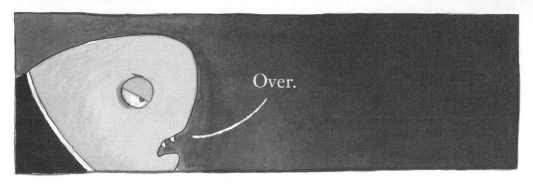

But it is!

Wolf made **EVERYTHING SEEM POSSIBLE.**

Without him, we're just

A BUNCH OF CROOKS.

And without him leading the way . . .

. . . you feel lost.

I get it. But . . .

No buts!

There's *nothing* you can say to make this better, *señorita*.

The **ALIENS** have taken over the world,

Wolf is **TOO BIG** and **TOO LOCO** to be stopped,

and **ALL HOPE IS LOST!**

Full respect to you and the League of Heroes, but *no one in the world could make this seem OK!*

Someone could.

Wolf could.

You're right, man.
We were nothing without Wolf.
But now . . .

. . . we're *something*
because of Wolf.

And just because he's
**KNOCKING DOWN
SKYSCRAPERS** with his bare hands
and **PARTYING WITH THE ALIENS,**
it doesn't give us the right
to give up.

Do you think *he'd* give up?

Or do you think he'd open his **BIG, STUPID MOUTH** and say something idiotic like . . .

"Hey, Piranha! You've got **SUPER SPEED!** That's a big deal, *hermano*!"

Or . . . "Shark! You're a **SHAPE-SHIFTER,** dude! Disguise yourself as something that will get us out of this mess!"

Or . . . "Legs! What do we do here? You're the smartest **NON-VELOCIRAPTOR** I know!"

He really is!

And then he'd say,
"Aren't you all forgetting the

INTERNATIONAL LEAGUE OF HEROES?"

Finally.

"They are the **BEST OF THE BEST!**"

Yes, we are.

And so are we!

Uh, no.
No, that's . . .
No.

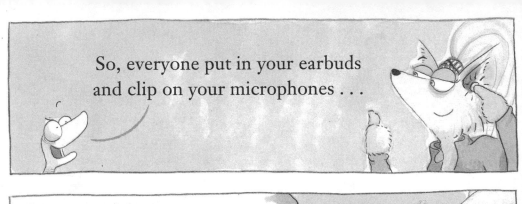

So, everyone put in your earbuds and clip on your microphones . . .

This is how it's going down:

HALF OF US need to keep going with **OPERATION TARANTULA.** We need to get our eight-legged buddy and Agent Shortfuse onto that **MOTHER SHIP.** Legs has to **TAKE CONTROL** of that thing. It's the only way we'll stop those aliens.

Half of us?!
But what do the
OTHER HALF do?

The other half will
be participating in
**OPERATION
FUR-BRAIN.**

It's time to get
our big, hairy
buddy back.

· CHAPTER 2 ·
GOOD—BYE, FOR NOW

Your plan is to watch him **THROW BUSES?** What? Are you hoping he'll just get sore arms and take a power nap?

Doom,
give him a break.
Try again,
Mr. Snake . . .

*Wolf.
You WILL do
as I command . . .*

My **MIND POWERS** aren't working. He's **TOO BIG.** And he's **TOO FAR AWAY...**

And your mind powers aren't very good . . .

Cut it out, Joy.

Your name's *Joy*?!

I'll get you for this.

Oh, shush.

Mr. Snake, I think we need to **DISTRACT** Mr. Wolf, to **GET YOU CLOSER...**

Any ideas?

· CHAPTER 3 ·
NEW WINGS

OK, *listen up!*
That alien trash **BLEW UP MY JET,**
so we have to get ourselves one of those
ZIPPY LITTLE SPACESHIPS.
THAT'S how we get to the big one.

There's one!

We'll never get near it. There are too many aliens . . .

Too many?!
You're looking at the
piranha who defeated a
TYRANNOSAURUS REX!

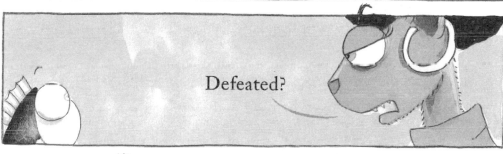

Defeated?

I thought you just got
**STUCK IN ITS
NOSTRIL . . .**

ENOUGH OF THIS TALK!
You must **"BORROW"
THAT SPACESHIP**
and save the world, *amigos . . .*

Well, what do
you want?
An invitation?

Let's "borrow" that
spaceship . . .

· CHAPTER 4 ·
IN ONE EAR...

MR. WOLF!

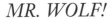

Mr. Wolf?
It's me. It's Agent Fox . . .

46

That sounds a little formal,
doesn't it? *Agent Fox.*
It's funny . . . I just realized . . .

I've never told you my
real name, have I?

Well, it's high time I did. Allow me
to introduce myself, Mr. Wolf.
My name is . . .

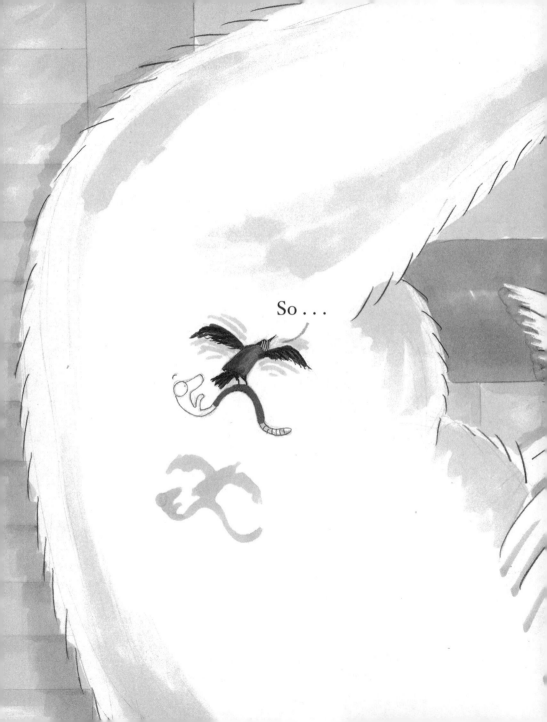

So . . .

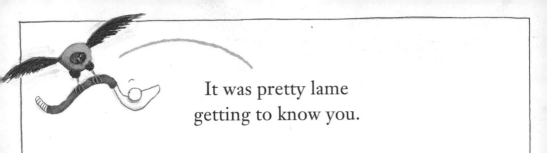

It was pretty lame
getting to know you.

Thanks.
I feel the same.

Try not to die,
I guess.

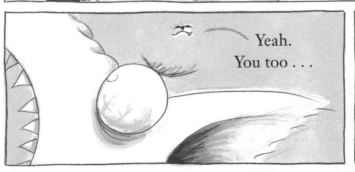

Yeah.
You too . . .

Joy.

I am SO out of here.

Thanks for the ride.

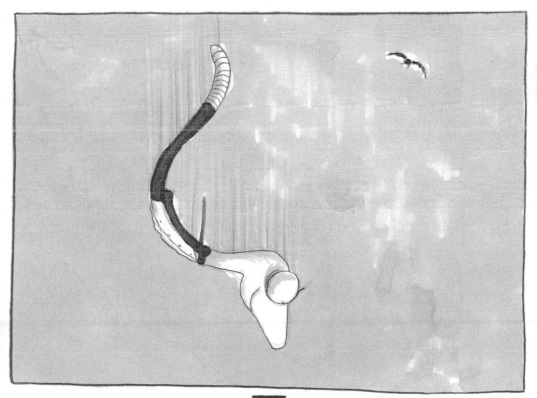

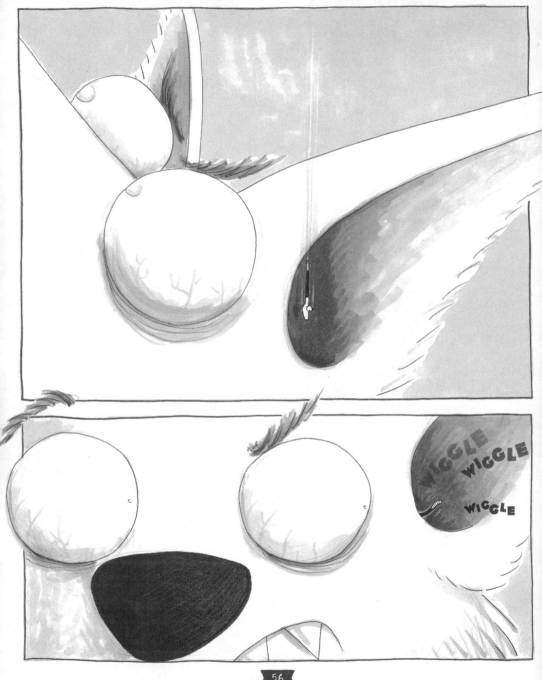

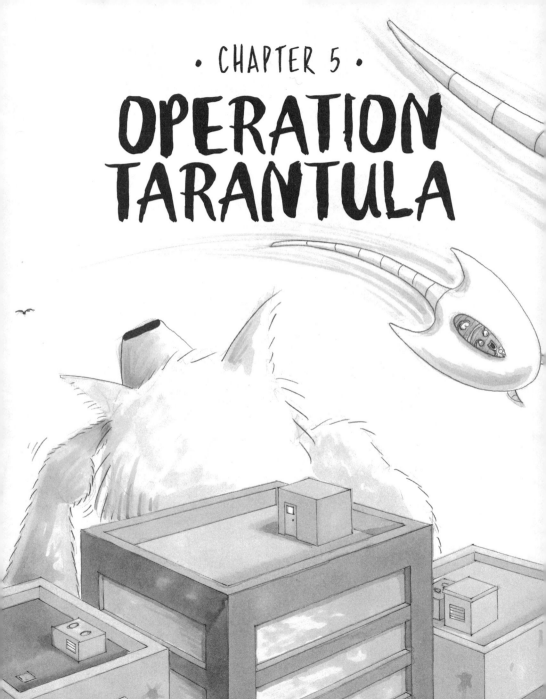

Not with *you* flying!
Give me that stick,

LITTLE MISS MUFFET.

But . . .
I've only been teaching
you for about thirty seconds . . .

flick!

Well, guess what?
It's **GRADUATION DAY!**
MOVE IT!

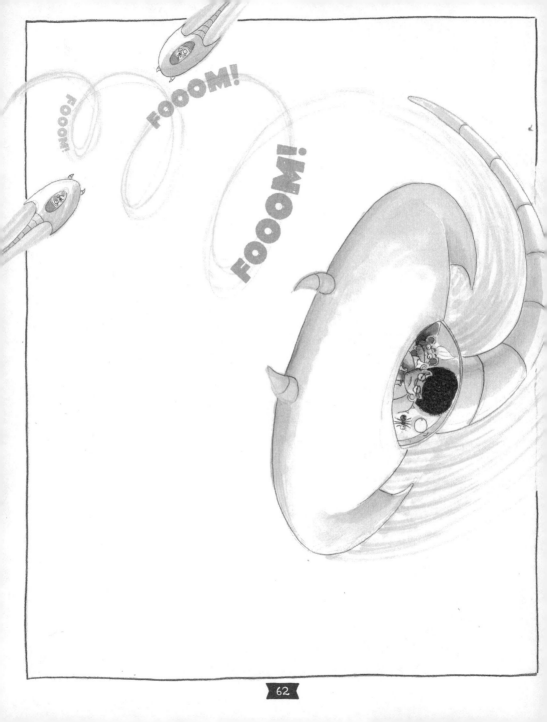

She's a really fast
learner . . .

Now GET INTO YOUR CONTAINER!
I'm going to launch you onto
the mother ship from the
GARBAGE CHUTE.

But won't they see us launch?
We'll be sitting ducks . . .

You know I am.
It's time to shine, baby . . .

Well, *giddyup* . . .

Do it quick! We're almost there,
but they're all over us . . .

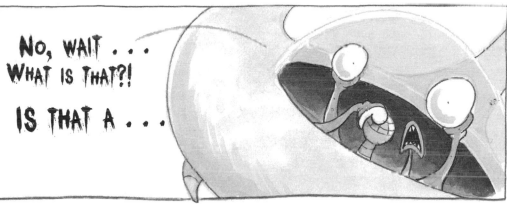

BLOW IT OUT OF THE SKY!

COPY THAT.
SHOOTING THE
UNICORN ON THREE.

ONE . . .

Here goes nothing . . .

GULP!

FOOOOP!

PTOOOEEEYY!!!!

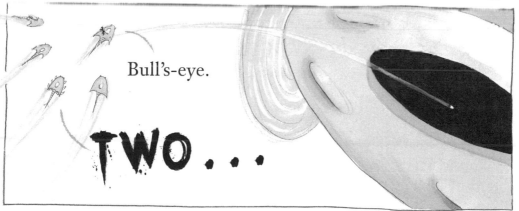

Bull's-eye.

TWO . . .

THREE!

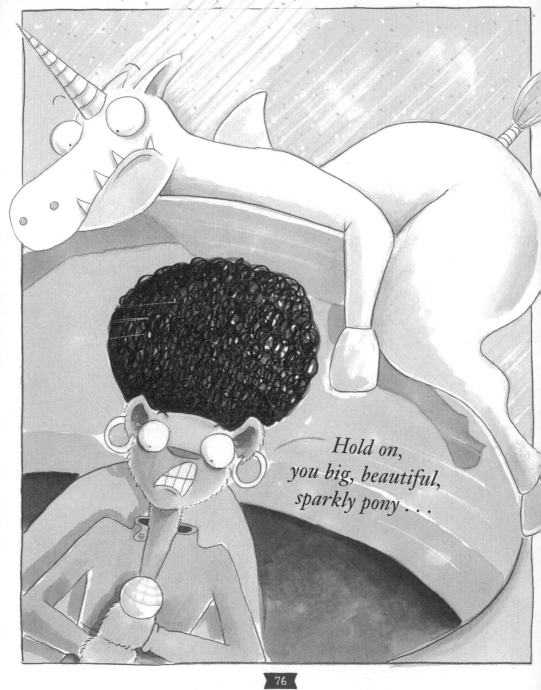

WE'RE GOING DOWN!

· CHAPTER 6 ·
THE WOLF WHISPERER

Oh man.
This is disgusting.

You *WILL* stop this.
You *WILL* calm down.
You *WILL* return to normal.

Mr. Snake? Can you hear me?
Just KEEP AT IT!

I can't do it . . .

Just *try*. You have to try.

Soooo sorry to interrupt,
but I fear we may have a teensy-
weensy **PROBLEM** . . .

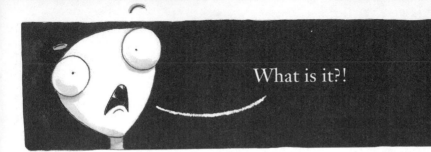

Well. I just upgraded to some high-quality **HEADPHONES** because those little **EARBUDS** you're all wearing won't be comfortably accommodated by my **PRIMORDIAL EAR HOLES.**

It's been quite a trial.

But fear not, these new ones

are really quite excellent . . .

HOW IS THIS RELEVANT?!

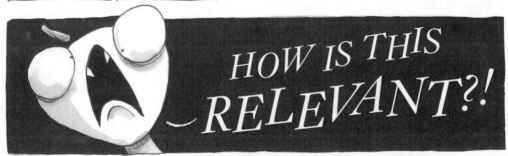

Well, that's the thing. These headphones are of such a high standard that they seem to have picked up on

ANOTHER SIGNAL

coming from Mr. Wolf's enormous head.

What kind of signal . . . ?

Well. Unless I'm *very* much mistaken, I suspect there's

SOMEONE ELSE

lurking about in his

OTHER EAR.

Marmalade?!

WOLF!
EAT THAT FOX AND
DESTROY THIS CITY!
NOW!

· CHAPTER 7 ·
WHO NEEDS SUPERPOWERS?

Not bad, Agent Hogwild.
We make a pretty good team.

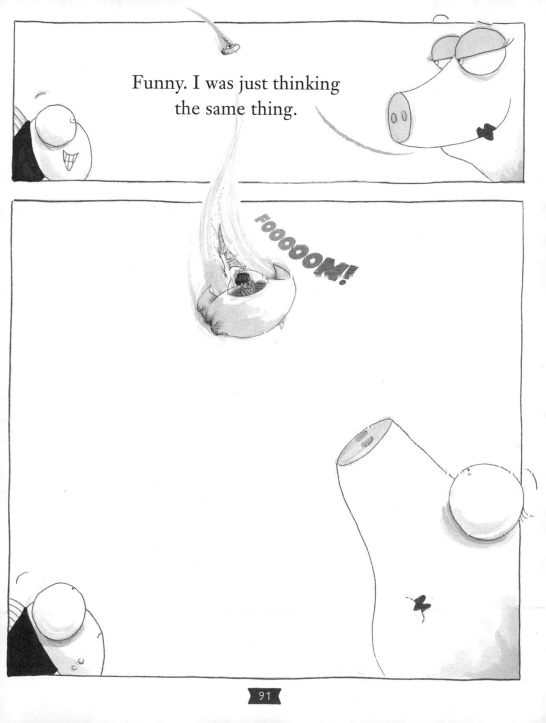

Was that a . . . *UNICORN*?!

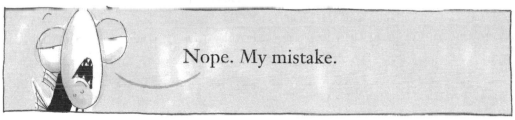

Nope. My mistake.

HELP!

Welcome back, guys, but we'd better move. **FOX IS IN TROUBLE . . .**

Thank goodness you're here!
Things have taken a
turn for the worse . . .

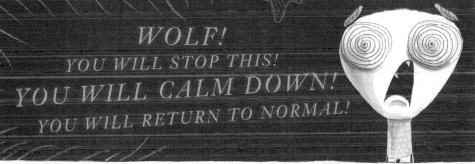

Fox?
It's hopeless.

I can't reach him.

Will you try something for me?

What?

Forget you have mind powers for a minute.
Just pretend you're

PLAIN OLD MR. SNAKE.

WHAT?
What good will that do?!

That way you can just talk to him.
He loves you.
Just . . . *talk to him.*

But that's . . .

Hey, Wolf?

Yeah I'm talking to *you*, Butt Brain.

Look, man, enough's enough. I'm waist-deep in earwax here,

and my patience has **RUN OUT.**

What you're doing is **BAD.** Do you hear me?

You're behaving like a **BAD GUY.**

And at this point, that is *very* disappointing, dude.

So for our sake, and for the sake of

everything you've worked for . . .

I need you to **CUT IT OUT.**

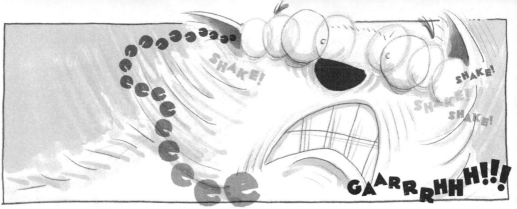

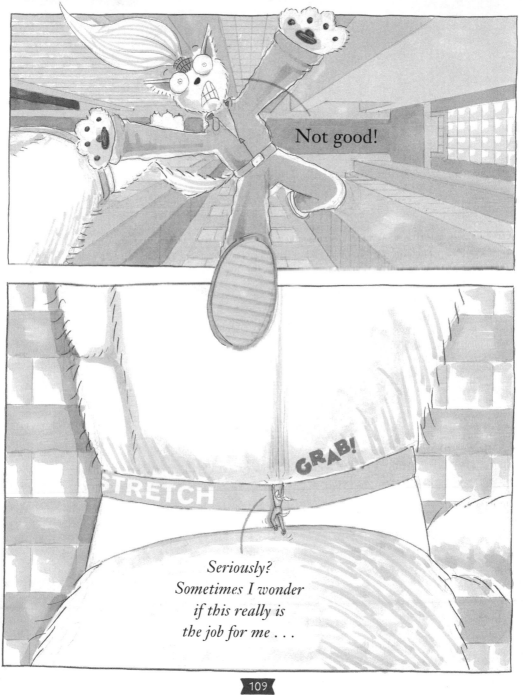

But you're also the best thing
that's ever happened to me.

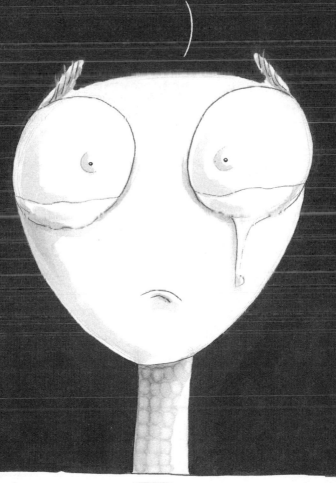

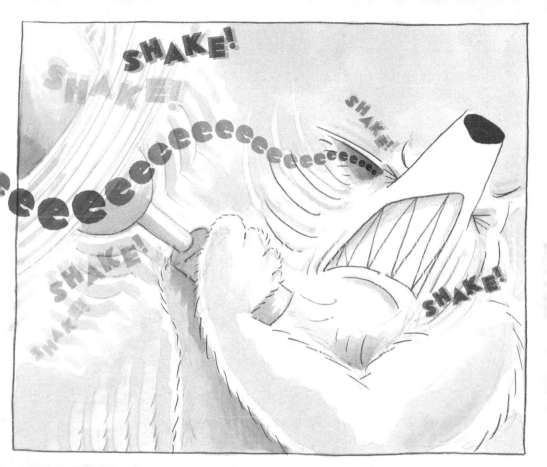

Ah!
That's
lucky . . .

Mr. Wolf?!

Oh, Mr. Wolf.
It's *you*!

Agent Fox . . . What . . .
What have I done?!

• CHAPTER 9 •
THE DARKEST HOUR

 *That's it, Butt Hands!* Let's blast up there and take him down!

Whaaa . . . wait a minute! My **SUPER SPEED** . . . it's . . .

Gone. So is my power. **I CAN'T CHANGE.** He must have taken it all away with that weird blast.

And why's he wearing a **CROWN** all of a sudden?

 **GREAT** QUESTION! YOU MUST BE **BUSTING** TO ASK ME SO MANY THINGS.

. . . OH YES,
OF COURSE . . .

YOUR LITTLE BUDDY
MR. SNAKE IS GONE
FOREVER!

TO BE CONTINUED . . .

NOOOOOOO!

The bad guy can't win!

THE BAD GUYS have to win!

This is the one you've been waiting for—

the **BAD GUYS**

in

The Baddest Day Ever!

Psst!
Hey, guys? We're here . . .
we made it onto the mother ship.
Guys?!
Uh . . . guys?